D1371006

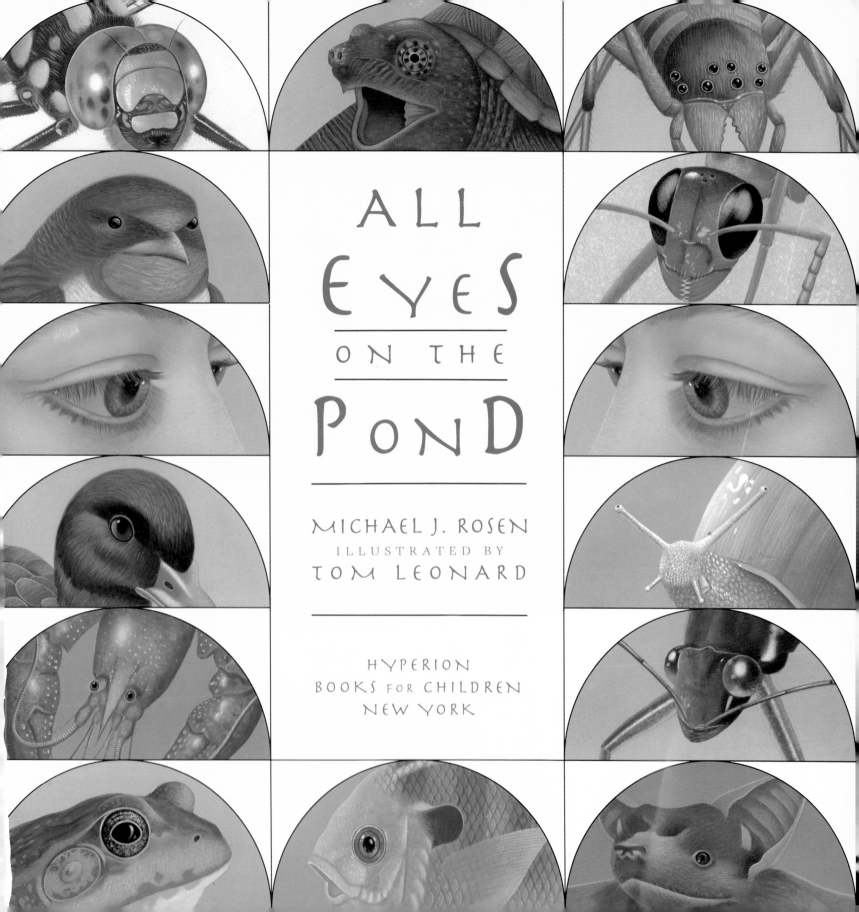

ALL EYES

ON THE

POND

MICHAEL J. ROSEN

ILLUSTRATED BY
TOM LEONARD

HYPERION
BOOKS FOR CHILDREN
NEW YORK

Here and there around this pond,

countless eyes watch what goes on.

Listen. They're all calling you:

Come closer, look! Come see my view.

A world of water multiplies

within the eyes of dragonflies,

whose gazes are kaleidoscopes

that spy atop the cattail slopes.

The snapping turtle sometimes sees

the muddy deep, sometimes the trees,

and sometimes nothing but inside

the painted shell where it can hide.

From where the spider always clings

the view is largely tangled things

dangling in the crisscrossed strands

that weave the windows where it stands.

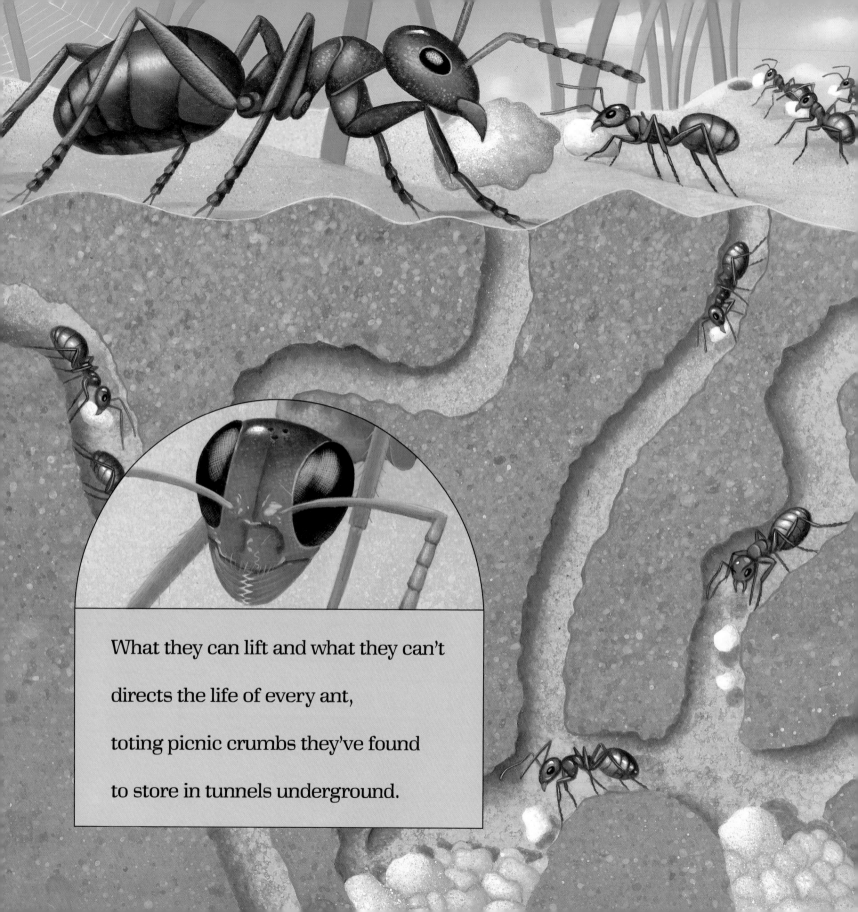

What they can lift and what they can't

directs the life of every ant,

toting picnic crumbs they've found

to store in tunnels underground.

The snail sees simply what it's on

as it glides up a stalk or frond.

Where next? The snail can still decide

as it glides down the other side.

The water strider walks the shine

where air and water form a line.

What's up above? What's down below?

It never has the chance to know.

With echoes bouncing through the night,

the bat can see without its sight.

Soundless shadows, hidden prey —

a bat may swoop and snatch away.

To what's ahead, the crawdad's blind.

It only sees what's left behind.

Whooshing backward by its tail,

the crawdad leaves a cloudy trail.

Peering toward the breezy air

where clouds are what the branches bear,

the bluegill watches at the brink

the flitting things it hopes will sink.

There…beside the fallen log,

the yellow peepers of a frog

who waits beside an old tree trunk,

nabs a fly, and jumps, *kerplunk*.

Paddling through the cattail shoots,

lily pads and toppled roots,

a mallard dips and dives and dunks

to munch upon the duckweed clumps.

Chittering swallows skitter so fast

and skim the waves as they soar past,

keeping an eye on all that's afloat —

a branch, a beetle, an anchored boat.

The pond itself, seen from the sky,

appears to be a giant's eye.

What's it watching, staring back?

A storm? The clouds? The zodiac?

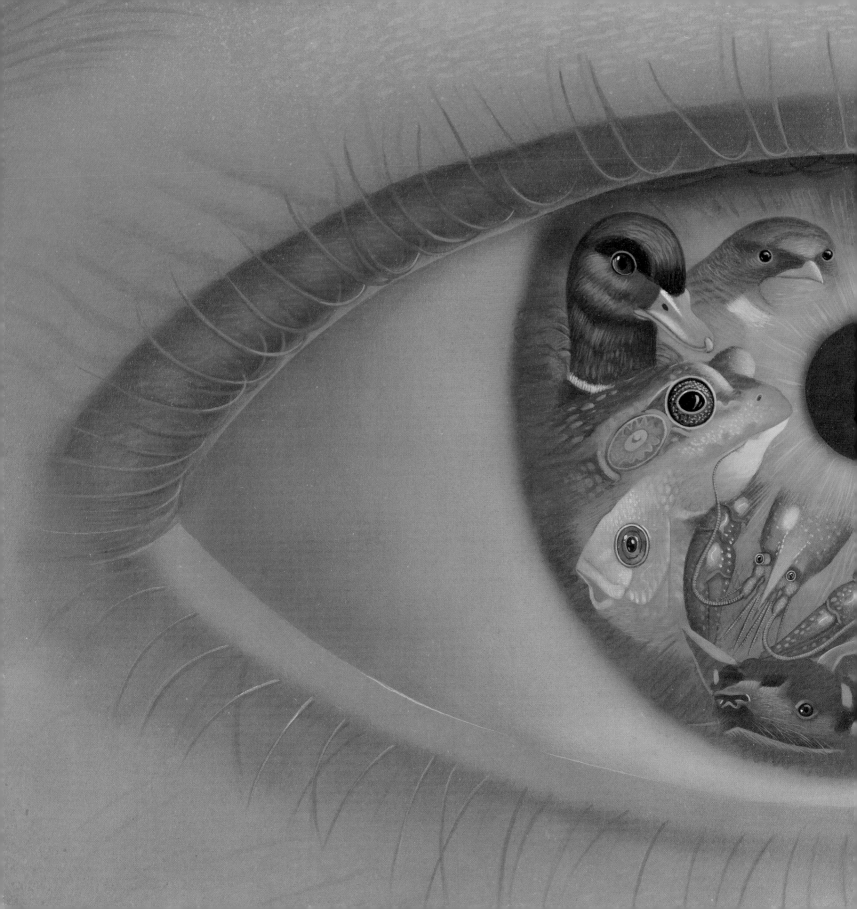

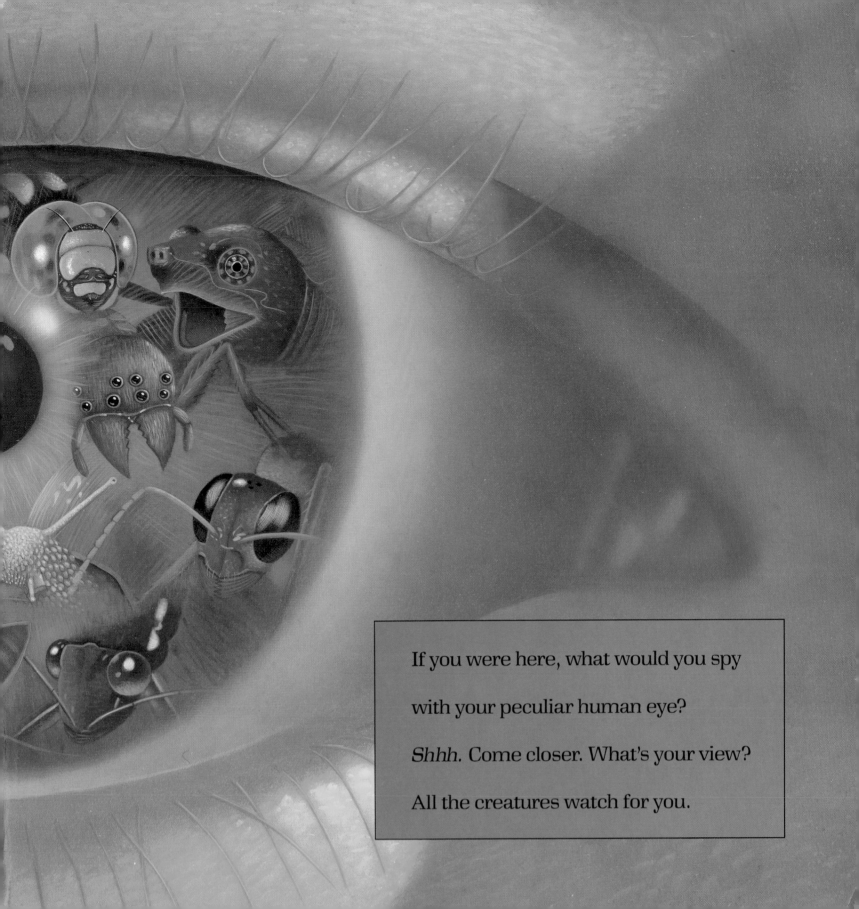

If you were here, what would you spy

with your peculiar human eye?

Shhh. Come closer. What's your view?

All the creatures watch for you.

TO MY NEPHEW, LOUIS
-M. J. R.

FIRST EDITION
1 3 5 7 9 10 8 6 4 2

Library of Congress Cataloging-in-Publication Data
Rosen, Michael J.
All eyes on the pond/Michael J. Rosen; illustrated by Tom Leonard — 1st ed.
p. c.m.
ISBN 1-56282-475-9 (trade) — ISBN 1-56282-476-7 (lib. bdg.)
1. Pond fauna — Juvenile literature. [1. Pond animals.]
I. Leonard, Thomas, ill. II. Title.
QL 146.3.R67 1994
591.92'9 — dc20   93-11743   CIP   AC

The text is set in 17-point Antikva Margaret.

The artwork for each picture is prepared using acrylic on illustration board.